THRESHOLD

BY

DR. SOMA DUTTA

ISBN 978-93-5438-071-6

Published in India 2020 by Pencil

A brand of

One Point Six Technologies Pvt. Ltd.

123, Building J2, Shram Seva Premises,

Wadala Truck Terminal, Wadala (E)

Mumbai 400037, Maharashtra, INDIA

E connect@thepencilapp.com

W www.thepencilapp.com

Author biography

About the Author

Dr. Soma Dutta is the Founder President of PGF World Literary & Cultural Foundation, a registered N.P.O. under the Ministry of Corporate Affairs. She is the Chief Editor of the magazine 'Aspirations'.

Dr. Soma Dutta is the author of several books of Literature and History. She composed innumerable poems, many of which have been published as books, in magazines, journals etc. She also wrote short stories, Articles, a Novel and a History book.

Dr. Soma Dutta is an Educationist by prefession. She worked in many reputed schools of the country, first as a teacher and then as a Principal. At present she has been working as the Principal of Future Pride International School, Greater Noida.

Dr. Dutta won many prizes and awards for her praiseworthy contribution in the field of Education, Social work and Literature at the District, State and National levels. She is the Author of Eleven books. She has been associated with the field of education for more than thirty years .Her favourite quote in life is " Miles to go before I sleep."

Contents

FOREWORD

About the Book

T hreshold is a book of poems which contains poems reflecting various moods, thoughts and expressions. It is a blend of emotions and reality. Most of the poems have been composed during the Lockdown period and in a challenging time when the whole world is being affected with Corona Virus Pandemic. Fear of disease and death can compel us to stay at home, confined within the four walls of our house. But no one can force our thoughts, our creative zeal to remain confined to our mind. Every moment , mind creates them and sets them free to reach the hearts of others.These thoughts take the shape of poetry and waits at the threshold to cross the line and spread their wings in the open air.

Threshold is that symbol of freedom which is sure to touch the enlightened minds. As it has been rightly said, Literature is a mirror of the society, it has the power to reform the society also . Poetry is a very important and effective weapon of Literature in this mammoth task of social reform. Again, poetry touches a million minds with emotion, depth of feelings, expressions hidden behind the words.

Threshold is expected to win the heart of its readers. The book is being dedicated to all the poetry lovers of the world.

INTRODUCTION

CONTENTS

VIRUS MENACE

Since ages, we were sleeping

Under the deep layers of ice,

We were confined there since ages,

But comfortable and alive

Although amidst breathless white haze.

Until one day, we felt a little warmth,

A faint ray of sunlight.

We heard the crack of ice

And its melting into water bright.

As if breaking the prison,

The convicts are coming out under the sky,

Perplexed by the sudden freedom.

We are crazy, hyperactive and our spirit is rising high.

We are grateful to humans,

It is their credit to bring us out.

Had they not created global warming,

We would have remained inactive, inert.

You have given us sweet names –

Ebola, Nipah, Corona,

You have destroyed our natural habitat.

Now let's take shelter in your arena,

You will remain in isolation,

With masks hiding half of your face,

We will rule in your body,

For several nights and days.

If you want to get rid of us,

Stop polluting the Earth.

Let us sleep under layers of ice,

Don't bring us out into the dearth.

IF I COULD GO BACK TO MY MOTHER

Mother came in my dream last night,

Clad in a sky colour Jamdani Sari,

Which was my favourite of all her dresses in my childhood,

In which she looked like a beautiful fairy.

She was sitting by the side of my bed,

Gently caressing my uncombed hair,

Her familiar smell filled my room,

The faint scent of lavender freshened up the air.

Her soothing touch healed my mind,

Relieved me of all my pain,

As if like quenching the thirst of a parched ground,

With a sudden spell of refreshing rain.

Again after a long time

I went back to those golden days,

When no other emotion could shake my mind,

Except profound trust and pure happiness.

Holding my hand she used to teach me

Alphabets, numbers and rhymes.

Writing on the slate with chalks

And reciting limericks and hymns.

She could understand which one is my real smile

And which one is just feigning.

She could read my face and mind,

Observing my expressionless eyes or their twinkling.

Life without mother was unthinkable then,

Bond between us was inseparable.

Her lap was the most secured place,

Her love, the most desirable.

I don't know when everything changed!

How we went far away from each other?

My destiny kept on changing my life,

I was introduced to another world without mother

With the arrival of new persons in my life,

Came duties and responsibilities,

Stress, workload and tensions.

Defeating childhood trust and peace,

The person who was dearest to me,

Gradually lost priority in every matter.

She remained in my mind like a precious ornament,

Which is kept in a treasure trove or a bank locker,

When she became old and lost her vigour,

I could neither feel nor understand,

Defeating my belief that she will never leave me,

She left, leaving footprints on the sand.

She came last night in my dream,

My mother, who had brought me on this Earth.

I was her dream, nurtured with care,

Which became a reality with my birth.

If I could go back once again

To my sweet childhood days,

When life was easy and simple

Free from anxiety and stress.

When there were no responsibilities,

Only playing around freely,

Mother was there to look after everything,

I enjoyed every moment daily.

Burdened by the shackles of duty,

Today when I look for her,

I can't find her address,

She is not to be found anywhere.

UNKNOWN WORLD

Have we started liking this?

Keeping distance, aloof from the society!

In a cocoon, a close-knit family,

Cut off from the moribund life of a city !

Simple life with minimum needs,

Ample time to say the unspoken words,

Holidays for an unlimited period,

Neither looking back nor forward

Sound of calling bell is rare now,

Its sudden sound scares the mind.

Are we becoming habituated to isolation?

Is it the slow evolution of mankind?

Life has come to a halt,

No further progress, no development.

Is it healing our mind and body?

Temporary phase seems to be permanent.

Carfew, Lockdown, Seal.......

These are now part of our life,

Gradually turning us stoic,

While time is sharpening its knife.

Shall we get back our normal life?

Before we forget the known faces

Of our neighbours and colleagues,

Our relatives and dear friends!!!

A big question mark on survival and existence,

Is the history of civilization getting destroyed?

We are helpless, silent observers,

For whose sin is this dreadful situation created?

We desired for a new world,

But not a sick world like this.

We wished for a positive change

But not at the cost of peace.

BLOOD DRENCHED INDEPENDENCE

Bloodshed has not stopped

Even after so many years of Independence,

We are celebrating 15th August every year,

With homage to the martyrs and our reverence.

Mother's lap becomes empty even now,

Her tears remain captured in her eyes,

She bids farewell to her brave son,

While her suppressed pain lingers in the skies.

In a country, where still the poor sleeps on the road,

Many do not get two square meals,

Crores are spent on defence,

Due to the greed of the neighbouring countries.

When after vacation, a soldier returns to the border,

Leaving behind his family members,

No one knows whether he will come back alive again,

Or in a coffin, draped in a Tri-colour!

Many young lives had embraced death,

While making the country free from the foreigners,

The intruders left, sowing the seeds of hatred,

Permanently in the minds of the neighbours.

Today, in our Independent India,

The Tri-colour is fluttering high in the air,

National song and Anthem reverberate everywhere,

The whole Nation celebrates together.

But no one can understand the feelings of

The infants who lost their father,

A newly married bride ,

who became a widow within a month,

A poverty stricken family

who lost their only earning member.

Independence was our most cherished dream,

Fulfilled after tearing the shackles of long slavery.

Protecting the borders is now a nightmare,

For those who are becoming victims of cruel treachery.

Independence will lose its value,

If this bloodshed continues endlessly,

If in our own land, we have to live with fear,

Surrendering before fate and destiny hopelessly.

INJUSTICE

In that country

Where stripping Draupadi of her clothes

Was not prevented by the brave and wise,

And Duryodhan was not penalized ......

In that country

Where abduction of Sita

Could not be resisted

But her chastity was questioned.....

In that country

Where candles are the only weapons

To condemn the rapists

And criminals are set free

For being juveniles

All raped and tortured girls who left this world,

Don't Rest in Peace.

Take revenge on the animals

Who extinguished the lamp of your life

Never spare them

They have no right to survive.

DIFFERENT WORLD

We fell asleep in one world

And woke up in another.

Suddenly Disneyland is out of magic,

Paris is romantic no longer.

Time Square has lost all glamour,

Niagra is falling down without any cheers,

The Pyramids don't fascinate anymore,

Rivers are flowing like tears.

Hugs and kisses are weapons,

Distance from all is expression of care.

Power, beauty and money are worthless,

These can't give you life saving air.

The world continues living,

Only it has put humans in cages.

Nature is more beautiful now,

And is sending us its messages.

"You are not necessary,

All elements of this planet are happy without you.

All birds and animals are free in your absence,

Plants and flowers are happy too.

When you come back again,

Remember, you are not my masters,

You'll be back only as guests,

Come back only with smile and laughter.

REALISATION

Living a hygienic life

Is not difficult at all,

We can survive without junk food

And trashes from the mall.

Eat less and be strong,

Don't be obese like the rich.

You will be healthy and wise,

If you practise what you preach.

Oil rich countries

Are now at the mercy of God.

Their wealth can't save them,

Time is really very odd.

Lockdown should have been imposed

On human greed long back.

Now forget modern lifestyle,

To the traditional life, go back.

LIFE IS A RIDDLE

I try to be a Panglossian,

When I go to sleep at night

And expect to see a disease-free world

In the morning, drenched with bright sunlight.

When we can give sweet cwtch

To our nearest and dearest ones.

Defenestrating all barriers

And enjoying all frolics and funs.

All are turning agathokakological,

No one is run-of-the-mill now.

Flabbergasted by the bizarre world,

Where a developing country helps

a developed one- WoW!

Believe me, no one is big or small,

This belief is not floccinaucinihilipilification.

We all are in the same boat brother,

"Stay home, stay safe"is our mission.

THE SIMPLEST

Do you think I have

Hippopotomonstrosesquipedaliophobia?

No dear, then you are an opsimath.

I am a scripturian, not a gonzo,

Attracted towards the language path.

Arcana of my journey in this field

Is my passion for apposite vocabulary.

I don't care for the snollygosters

And the floccinaucinihilipilification

Or Tomfoolery.

My words are never farrago,

Neither am I a rodomontade.

I am a simple and straightforward person,

Love English language with its varied shade.

FRIENDSHIP

Friendship is eternal,

Friends are forever.

It's not just for one day,

One month or a year.

It's a relationship of souls,

Thicker than blood relation.

Staying thousand miles away,

Friends remain close in any situation.

Friends tell us to hold fast to our dreams,

For if dreams die,

Life becomes a broken winged bird,

That can not fly.

MY FATHER

The person who taught me the name of the stars,

Pointing his fingers at the night sky,

Who told me about the different phases of the moon,

When it peeped through the trees high-

He is my father.

The person who instilled values in me,

And said, " Better fail than cheat."

Who taught me the realities of life,

And told me, "Winners never quit." –

He is my father.

The person who fulfilled all my childhood wishes,

Made me feel secured and safe,

Never ignored my dreams and aims,

But helped me to give them a shape-

He is my father.

The person who felt pride in me,

Was happy to be the father of a girl,

Never compared me with a boy

And treasured me like a pearl-

He is my father.

I don't know where he is today!

In which unknown, strange land!!!

I feel he is somewhere near me,

I feel the touch of his assuring hand.

I love you my father.

RAIN BE WITH ME

Rain stay with me and whisper in my ears,

Fan my cheeks with your gentle breeze,

Let your tiny droplets moisten my face,

And help me reminisce my childhood days with ease.

Today birds are silent in their hidden nests,

Butterflies are not fluttering their wings,

Squirrels have stopped twitching their tails,

All are listening to the melody which rain brings.

The intoxicating aroma of the wet soil,

The tune of Megh Malhaar in the air,

The misty veil of tranquility,

In a moribund life, is rare.

It's a day to lose oneself,

Breaking all norms and barriers.

Weaving the net of day dreams,

While rain dances with her silvery attires.

I AM A WOMAN

I am a woman, the best creation of God.

I am a part of the Nature,

I am tolerant like the Earth, strong like a mountain,

But delicate like a feather.

I am broad like the sky, fiery like the burning flame

And crystal clear like water.

Tears trickle down my one eye,

While pride reflects from the other.

I can sing lullaby, rocking my child's cradle.

Keeping a rock on my heart,

I can send the same child to the war front.

I am a loving, dutiful mother.

I lose myself, staring at the first monsoon drizzling.

I feel intoxicated when the autumn wind whispers in my ears.

I build my home with all my dreams and passions.

But when I face a threat to my little world,

I raise my voice, my kind eyes glare with anger.

With millions of poisonous hoods,

The snake in me can sting venom,

I am a woman, the best creation of God.

I shelter men in my womb for ten months,

Create and nurture them with my blood and milk.

I am the creator, the protector and if required, the destroyer too.

I kill all evil demons in men.

I awaken their conscience with a prick.

I am the poet's imagination.

With rhymes in ink on a blank sheet,

A splash of colours on a serene backdrop,

I am an artist's source of inspiration.

I am the brandishing sword in a warrior's hand.

An actor's real life expressions.

When I take birth,

Sometimes I am received with happiness,

Sometimes with sorrow and depressions.

But I have the strength to survive and stand on my feet,

To win the world and emerge victorious,

To consolidate my identity,ignoring all frustrations.

Iam a woman, the best creation of God.

I am a multi-tasker throughout different phases of my
life –

Daughter, sister, friend, lover, wife , mother and beyond.

Bent and wrinkled with experience,

I carry history forward

As past reverberates all around.

I am a woman, the best creation of God.

I have come to this Earth with a purpose.

God's specific assignments

are being accomplished by me,

The process of creation is being carried on by me,

If I get a chance to take birth again,

I will come on this Earth as a woman.

LIGHT A LAMP

Light a lamp in the heart of your nearer,

Light a lamp in the life of the poorer.

Light a lamp to remove the darkness of mind.

Light a lamp to awaken the divine.

Light a lamp to spread the light of knowledge,

Light a lamp to kindle the fire of courage.

Light a lamp to motivate the wise,

Light a lamp to help the fallen, rise.

SPRING

The aroma of an unknown wild flower

Intoxicates the silent bower.

Honeybees buzz in the air,

New leaves adorn the twigs,

Free birds spread their wings.

The festival of Spring is being celebrated by nature.

Cuckoos' call made an announcement of her arrival,

As Spring appeared in her flowery apparel.

The gentle southern breeze welcomed her,

The fragrance of flowers can be smelt in the air

Butterflies flutter their designed wings everywhere.

The Mango trees blossom to add to her splendour.

PROMISE OF A NEW INDIA

This day dawned with a different light,

A mesmerizing tune is lingering in the air.

As it blows across the land and water,

Touching all hearts with happiness to share.

When India had become Independent,

Indians were free from the bondage,

Became self- dependent, in spite of all limitations

And revived our lost tradition and heritage.

The martyrs taught us to keep our flag high,

Braving all challenges and hardships.

Our country is our pride and glory,

The Golden Bird of the past deserves our worships.

Independence has given us more responsibilities

To enhance the prestige of our country,

To make her existence safe and secured,

And ensure her glorious victory.

Come, my countrymen, let us take the pledge,

We will never bow our head before any injustice,

Never leave the path of truth and honesty,

Always raise our voice against any cruel practice.

We will create a new India,

Where no one will die of hunger,

No one will be deprived of knowledge

And people of all religions and castes will walk together.

LOVE'S DIFFERENT SHADES

Love's definition is still unknown,

It is different at different phases of life.

Starting with the bond between mother and child,

It grows with shades of diverse types.

Love overflows the brim of a family goblet,

Wrapped in the quilts shared by the siblings.

On the footpath, in a palace,

Everywhere, reflecting the same feelings.

In the bed time stories of grandparents

And classroom chats in whispers,

Love's bounty is abundant

In fathers' secured and safe shelters.

Love is romantic at times,

As warm breath fans the cheeks of lovers.

Sometimes passion intoxicates body and soul,

While Platonic love believes only in untouched powers.

Loving the creation is loving Nature,

Space, Earth, Fire, Water and Air.

Accepting everything to be our own

And embracing everything with equal love and care.

Above all is the love for our Motherland

Our freedom fighters embraced the hanging noose for her.

Our brave Army-men are sacrificing their lives

Their love for the country is rare.

Love is the elixir of life

Our only reason for surviving.

Deprivation of love makes our lives isolated,

Compelling us to seek for life's meaning.

SPRING SYMPHONY

Winter said,"Good Bye" that day

When I observed the dawn appeared earlier.

The misty blanket was no more

And all of a sudden I felt

A lot of activities everywhere.

The long hibernation period is over.

Tiny creatures started crawling out of their slumber.

The buzzing of bees,

The rustling of leaves,

The cuckoo's melodious song filled the afternoon air.

New leaves in the trees, new grass in the fields,

The Earth seemed to be clad in a beautiful attire.

Colourful flowers adorned the backdrops,

Intoxicating aroma boozed all senses

And butterflies with their fluttering wings

painted the nature.

Spring cleaning brought spring in my mind,

My house is now relieved of quilts,

blankets and woollens.

Although there is a chill in the morning air,

Still the dew drops sparkle on the carpet grass.

The coffee pots brew warmth of pure happiness.

Spring festival of colours came to the doorsteps,

All glooms were dispelled by the aura of festivity.

Splashing colours on the known and unknown,

The hidden child dropped the mask of adulthood.

Forgetting all ego and enmity,

Spring comes for a short time.

To gift us with life's elixir,

To rejuvenate the tired souls with her magic touch

Awakening in all, the rainbow of desire.

MAID OF THE MIST

As I look out of my bedroom window,

Into the misty evening sky

And observe the hide and seek of clouds in the horizon,

Against the backdrop of vermilion dusk

Thousand sounds of silence reverberates in my surroundings,

Making me nostalgic, kindling my emotion.

I see you before my eyes and closing my eyes.

You Maid of the Mist, mysterious, endless.

Your boisterousness, your edding steps,

The dancing diva, the epitome of beauty

Enlivening nature's bounty, ravishing Niagara,

God's best creation on the Earth, charming grace.

Crossing seven seas and innumerable rivers,

I had reached your bosom.

The Rainbow Bridge greeted with a smile,

Maple leaves fluttered from the other side.

Red and Blue raincoats made lovely motifs on water,

As I boarded the boat and stood on the isle.

I had never seen spectrum on water earlier,

I had never been so fearless on water.

You intoxicated me with your elixir,

You drenched me with millions of droplets

Draped me with your quilt of mist,

Filled me with thrill, joy and wonder.

The eternal landscape throughout the ages

Is a witness of your mesmerizing beauty.

Spreading cool serenity and peace,

You are incredible yet a reality.

A perennial fountain of life,

Nature's unique creation,

You are a heavenly bliss.

TUSU PARV

Tusu folk song reverberates on Kankshabati's bank,

As Adivasi women sing in unison and dance,

Holding each others' hands.

Morning sun adorns the sky and water with vermilion red,

Tusumani is taking leave from the tribal lands.

She is being immersed in Kankshabati

Amidst tribal songs and folk music.

The colourful, brightly decorated chaudalas,dolls and artifacts

Float for a while, as joy is at its peak.

"Go Tusu go, we have seen your love

My heart is not satisfied.

No fire is ignited by your love,

My hunger for love is not gratified."

Tusu is a domestic figure,

A member of rural household.

Legend says that she had sacrificed her life,

For the sake of her love, age old.

Tusu is inseparable from the lives of the tribals

Of Purulia, Birbhum, Midnapore and Bankura.

It is a festival of love and harvesting

With a riot of colours and mirthful aura.

The festival starts in December

And continues for a month,

Which is concluded on Makar Sankranti day

By women after a holi bath.

The rhythm of Madol and intoxication of Mahua

Make young suitors bold enough to propose

To express their love to unmarried girls

Who turn red in shame and at first refuse.

Somewhere mock fights, somewhere a witty repartee

On the eloquent banks of quiet Kankshabati river

The village fair throngs with neighbourhood tribals.

Same is the scene at Shilabati,

Subarnarekha and Dwarkeshwar.

Sweets made of newly harvested rice and jiggery

Are relished by the simple Adivasis.

Far away from the curse of civilization,

They live with poverty, joy and peace.

The married women pray for their husband's love

Flaunting their bangles, bindi and trinklets,

Their hopes, desires, wishes and dreams

Everything is deeply rooted to their faith.

Toshali Devi, who originated in the hills of Shushunia,

Is the most adorable Tusu of the tribals

She comes back every year in their thatched, mud huts.

And is worshipped on decorated chaudalas.

The coolest day of January

Could not dampen the spirit of the devotees.

Their simple life and pure happiness exist even today.

Far from the artificialities of the civilized cities.

SMALL WONDER

When my cute little grandson waved his tiny hand

And went beyond my vision with his parents

For security check and other formalities

Leaving us and the country behind,

I felt a lump in my throat, controlling my emotions.

A void was created in my mind, losing all responsibilities.

Is it possible for me to live on this Earth, without them?

Particularly the child, a piece of my heart !

Whose every activity is so adorable to me.

Whose innocent smile made my days so special,

Whose voice played music to my ears.

In his absence, how dull my life would be !

I don't remember how I spent the next few days,

Nights just followed the days and days chased the nights.

I was almost inert, as if devoid of life.

My cravings for taking him on my lap,

Planting innumerable kisses on his forehead

Obsessed my mind, till I came to know about Skype.

My son told me, I could fulfil my wish

Through a small web cam fixed to my laptop.

Getting connected through Skype or Messenger,

A new device for communication,

Another wonderful invention of the 21st century

Bridging the gap between far and near.

When I saw him first on the screen,

His heavenly smile and inquisitive eyes,

And heard his soft voice calling me "Granny",

A delightful thrill throbbed my heart.

An overwhelming emotion filled my mind,

Making my world bright and sunny.

He was so happy to see me,

He touched the screen and tried to touch me

He wanted to pour out his heart before me,

Shared all his experiences of the new place

His apartment, friends, neighbours

With his childish enthusiasm and energy.

I felt modern world has created a distance

And broken close – knit families

With the migration of nearest and dearest members

But modern civilization blessed us with inventions,

Created a link between two persons

Living thousands of miles away from each other.

LIFE AT SIXTY

Completing major part of the journey of our life,

Now we are standing on a bridge,

Between our previous and the next generations.

Our parents have either left the world

Or are waiting for the last ferry, to reach their
destination.

We are desperately relishing the taste of life

And wish this to continue forever.

But immortal time never listens

To the appeal of the mortals.

Now we are neither exuberant teenagers

Nor are we desperate young.

We are not even depressed old.

We are like calm, serene early winter landscape,

Enriched with memories and experience

We are neither heart- broken by sorrow

Nor carried away by unleashed happiness.

We know, silver lining do not shine around all clouds,

Fragrance of love is not found in all Gulmohars.

We have understood, there is an end of a new beginning.

We are neither jealous of anyone

Nor competitors of each other.

Still tears sometimes blur our vision,

As we swallow a lump of pain very artfully.

But next moment, a message or a phone call

Brings smile on our lips.

Dispelling the fog, like white , floating Autumn clouds.

Sometimes we meet, just for the sake of meeting,

Talking, singing, reminiscing , filling our heart with fresh air,

We walk forward towards the end.

Our children are now grown up, busy in their life,

Grandchildren are also learning the lessons of life.

Getting a rare opportunity,

Sometimes, we tell them our childhood stories

Which , once ,our parents and grandparents used to tell us.

And thus, keep alive the tradition.

TIME

Time doesn't wait for anyone.

Looking at the old mansion, I remembered this.

No one to light lamps in the evening,

No one to uproot the weeds

Which have engulfed the once beautiful garden.

Deep sighs are coming out of the broken pillars,

The witnesses of the good, old days.

When songs and laughters reverberated

And filled the air and the place.

Today the house is on the verge of demolition,

Along with many dreams and desires of the past.

History and glory of long back

Peep through the accumulated dust.

Future will wipe away the last reminiscent

In its place will stand a multi storeyed apartment.

Old has to go and make room for the new,

This is the bitter truth of life, harsh predicament.

FROM RIPPLES TO WAVES

Tiny droplets of water

Make a big ocean,

Tiny letters create words

And mind expresses them through pen.

Passion and creative zeal unlimited,

Splash of lively, vibrant colours.

Nostalgic moments captured in frames,

Beautiful designs on blank papers.

From the depth of mind

To the white sea of paper

Down the memory lane.

A lot of treasures to share.

Each word is wrapped in a passion

Each picture is draped in

The colours of emotion.

Creation is a painful process

But an eternal bliss.

When it is born with grace,

It spreads pure joy and profound peace.

From ripples to waves

It touches minds in various ways.

The tiny scribbling of ink

Can brighten up our gloomy days.

WE WILL MEET AGAIN

We will meet at the end of the pandemic,

We will meet when no one will be sick.

We will meet when the virus will sleep,

We will meet when no one will weep.

We will meet at the end of the dark night,

We will meet on a new dawn bright.

We will meet when Science will win,

We will meet in a world lush green.

We will meet with shaking hands,

We will meet on fecund lands.

We will meet without any fear,

We will meet with all friends dear.

We will meet when everything will be like before,

We will meet in the open outdoor.

We will meet without mask on our face,

We will meet with all charm and grace.